Who's Got the Etrog?

This
PJ BOOK
belongs to

_____

_____

pj Library®

JEWISH BEDTIME STORIES and SONGS

For Kameron, my expert sukkah builder
—J. K.

To J, my little funny human
—E.

KAR-BEN PUBLISHING, INC.
A division of Lerner Publishing Group, Inc.
241 First Avenue North
Minneapolis, MN 55401 USA
1-800-4-KARBEN

Website address: www.karben.com

Main body text set in Billy Infant Regular 18/24.
Typeface provided by SparkyType.

Library of Congress Cataloging-in-Publication Data

Names: Kohuth, Jane, author. | Elissambura, illustrator.
Title: Who's got the etrog? / by Jane Kohuth ; illustrated by Elissambura.
Other titles: Who has got the etrog?
Description: Minneapolis : Kar-Ben Publishing, [2018] | Series: Sukkot & Simchat Torah |
    Summary: When Auntie Sanyu celebrates Sukkot at her home with family and animal
    friends who are Ugandan Jews—the Abayudaya—Warthog will not let go of the
    etrog. Includes glossary and facts about the Abayudaya.
Identifiers: LCCN 2017030091 | ISBN 9781541509665 (lb) | ISBN
    9781541509672 (pb) | ISBN 9781541524095 (eb pdf)
Subjects: | CYAC: Stories in rhyme. | Etrog—Fiction. | Sukkot—
    Fiction. | Animals—Fiction. | Jews—Uganda—Fiction. |
    Uganda—Fiction.
Classification: LCC PZ8.3.K826 Who 2018 | DDC
    [E]—dc23

LC record available at https://lccn.loc.
    gov/2017030091

PJ Library Edition ISBN 978-1-5415-0968-9

Manufactured in Hong Kong
1-43946-33967-3/13/2018

091827.6K1/B1263/A4

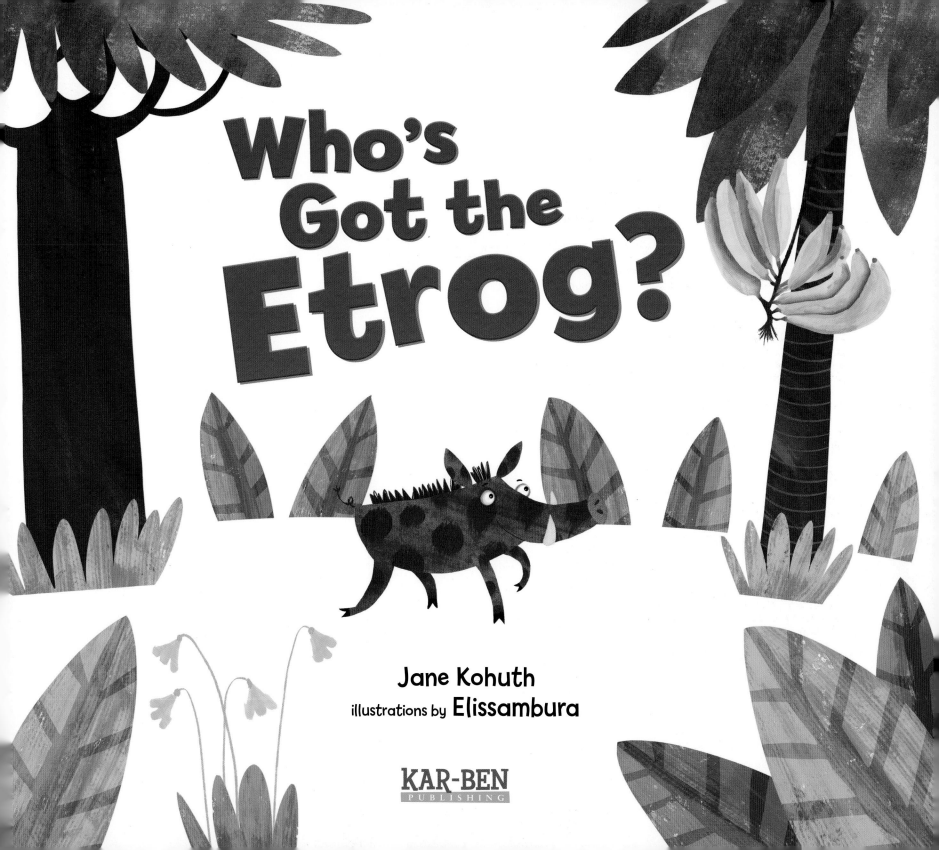

Who's Got the Etrog?

Jane Kohuth

illustrations by Elissambura

KAR-BEN
PUBLISHING

Auntie Sanyu's garden glowed beneath a milkbowl moon.
She picked ripe vegetables and fruit—Sukkot was coming soon!

It was time to build the sukkah. It took her three long days.
She hung plantains and paper chains and asked her friends to stay.
Then last she placed the lulav and the etrog on a tray.

On the first day, Warthog came to stay.
He ate his food politely
and shook the lulav gently.

Then he sniffed the Etrog—it smelled so good you know.
So round and yellow like the sun—he couldn't let it go!

On the second day, Lion came to stay.
Lion purred so nicely,
and Warthog ate politely.

They shook the lulav side to side, waved it to and fro.
But Warthog squeezed the etrog! He wouldn't let it go.

On the third day, Parrot came to stay.
She perched and said, "Shalom!" quite brightly,
while Lion rumble-purred so nicely,
and Warthog ate and drank politely.

Then they waved the lulav gently, shook it high and low.
But Warthog clutched the etrog! He wouldn't pass it, no.

On the fourth day, Camel came to stay.
She sipped her soup precisely,
while Parrot chatted brightly.
Lion purred so nicely,
and Warthog ate politely.

Each waved the lulav gently, shook it ground to sky,
but Warthog kept the etrog! Camel breathed a sigh.

On the fifth day, Giraffe came to stay.
He chewed leaves and listened quietly.
Camel sipped her soup precisely.
Parrot flapped and chatted brightly.
Lion rumble-purred so nicely.
Warthog passed the food politely.

They took turns with the lulav. They shook it west to east.
But Warthog grabbed the etrog! And Camel muttered,

BEAST!

On the sixth day, Rhino came to stay.
She danced with Auntie joyfully!
Giraffe watched very quietly,
while Camel sipped precisely,
and Parrot chatted brightly.
Lion purred so nicely,
and Warthog ate politely.

They waved the lulav gently.
They shook it every way.
But Warthog snatched the etrog!
And Camel cried,

OY VEY!

On the seventh day, Sara came to stay.
She visited her Auntie every holiday.

Rhino spun her joyfully.
Giraffe nodded quietly.

Camel shook her hand precisely.
Parrot said, "Shalom!" quite brightly.
Lion rubbed her knee so nicely,
and Warthog stood and bowed politely.

Then they passed the lulav. They waved it head to toe.
But guess who had the etrog?

Who wouldn't let it go?

Camel spat and Parrot squawked,
Rhino stamped and Giraffe gawked.

Lion snarled not very nicely.
"Hush," said Auntie Sanyu lightly.

"Let me hold the etrog," Sara said to Warthog gently.
"You can do it, Warthog. Let the etrog go."
She made him feel so sheepish, he couldn't tell her "No."

Then Warthog **SHARED** the etrog, and the guests all cried,

BRAVO!

On the eighth day, the friends gathered to pray. They asked for rain at home, and in Israel far away.

Then, so glad to be together, they twirled and leapt up high.
They spun and stomped and fluttered—and, at last, they said

GOOdbYE!

But then who spied the etrog, tucked away just so?

Yes, Warthog **HUGGED** the etrog—

and then he let it go!

Auntie Sanyu wrapped it carefully and said, "What do you say?
Shall we give Warthog the etrog?"
And the guests cried,

YES
HOORAY!

Sara and Auntie Sanyu called, "Chag sameach, friends, goodbye!"
Then they curled up on a blanket to watch the starry sky.

Glossary

Etrog: A lemon-like citrus fruit with a delicious scent that is used as part of the Sukkot holiday ritual.

Chag sameach: Hebrew for "happy holiday."

Lulav: A Sukkot item consisting of three types of branches: a palm branch, a willow branch, and a myrtle branch. It is used along with the etrog as part of the Sukkot holiday ritual.

Oy, vey!: A Yiddish expression of dismay. (Perhaps Camel picked this up from some European friends, as African Jews do not speak Yiddish.)

Shalom: Hebrew for "hello," "goodbye," and "peace."

Shemini Atzeret: Often considered the eighth day of Sukkot, Shemini Atzeret is a festival during which the Jewish people pray for rain in the land of Israel to help the crops grow.

Sukkot: Jewish harvest festival as well as a holiday commemorating the years spent wandering the desert before entering the Promised Land of Israel.

Sukkah: A temporary hut with a loosely woven roof through which one can see the stars. A sukkah is meant to resemble the huts Jews once built as they wandered in the desert, as well as the huts Jews built at harvest time when they worked in the fields. People often decorate the sukkah with hanging fruits and vegetables, paper chains, pictures, and other types of ornaments.

The history of the Abayudaya

The Jews of Uganda go back to the early 1900s to an unusual African chief named Semei Kakungulu. This warrior king decided to reject the Christian Bible that had been taught to him by missionaries traveling in Africa, and instead to follow only the first five books of the Bible—the Torah. Eventually Kakungulu's followers and descendants became accepted as Jews and the grandson of one of the chief's first followers came to America where he trained to become a rabbi, and returned to Uganda to lead its Jewish community.

Maccabee Yuda, a 16-year-old Abayudaya boy, teaching Hebrew at the synagogue in Nabugoya, Uganda.